IN THE KINGDOM OF MESCAL

In the Kingdom of Mescal

A fairy-tale for adults
told by Georg Schäfer
with illustrations by Nan Cuz
foreword by
Miguel Ángel Asturias
translated by Dinah Livingstone

Shambala Publications, Inc.
Berkeley 1970

SHAMBALA PUBLICATIONS, INC.
2010 Seventh Street · Berkeley, California 94710
ISBN 0-87773-016-4 · First Edition 1970
Copyright 1968 Carl Schünemann Verlag Bremen
English Translation Copyright 1969 McDonald Publishers, Ltd.
Originally published in German under the title
IM REICHE DES MESCAL
by Carl Schünemann Verlag Bremen
Printed in Germany.

Pictures and text are combined in this beautiful book to give us a magical vision of the American Indian world. Sound and colour create a reality enmeshed in dreams.
We are in the supernatural world of children and primitive peoples.
The close collaboration of the two authors Georg Schäfer and Nan Cuz is founded upon the depths of their personal feelings. These are the source of their understanding of the mysterious Indian world and of the beauty of their work. They have succeeded in creating a new dimension, that which is sought by art but not always found.
Let us take up this book to share in the human warmth of two great personalities, author Georg Schäfer, and painter Nan Cuz.

MIGUEL ÁNGEL ASTURIAS

Paris, May 1968

Once upon a time in a sunny country there lived a small boy with his father, who was a fisherman. His mother called him Blackhair because his hair was blacker than the blackest night.

Blackhair was a dreamer and his mother worried about him because instead of mending nets and collecting firewood from the great forest he lay on the river bank hour after hour and gazed up at the sky. "What is behind the stars?" he wondered. "Where does the kingdom of the gods begin and where does it end?"

Lost in such questions he forgot everything that his mother had told him to do. And even at night when he lay in his hammock he talked to the moon and did not fall asleep until it disappeared behind the forest mountains.

And in the morning the sun was up for many hours while Blackhair slept on.

One day his mother asked the old medicine man for advice, because she was very worried. The wise old man sent for Blackhair and said to him: "Be patient. I know what you want and you can have it." He went out of the hut and came back with a beautiful, richly decorated gourd. "Take this gourd," he said, "but be sure to look after what is inside it. When the moon shows its full face go out. Follow your heart, for it will lead you. But take care your head does not say: 'Follow me and not your stupid heart,' for then you will lose your way and may never come out of the forest ever again. When your heart tells you: 'This is the place,' stop and find somewhere to rest. Before the sun goes down, take the gourd and drink what is in it. Then you will find the way to the Kingdom of Mescal."

When the moon showed its full face, Blackhair took the brightly painted gourd, as he had been told, bowed to his parents who were asleep, and went out. He wandered through the maize fields and soon he stood before a thick green wall. As far as his eye could see grew row upon row of tree trunks, so high that they looked as if their green heads were trying to reach up and see the world of the gods enthroned above the clouds.

Underneath there was brushwood, and creepers as thick as a man's arm. The light shone through the trees of the primeval forest and coloured everything a mysterious green.

On the ground Blackhair saw wonderful flowers, more beautiful than any he had seen before. Now and then he heard something rustling nearby, or the monkeys chattering in the treetops. "Blackhair," his head warned him, "go back Blackhair, there is still time."

"Remember what you have come for," said his heart. "Stand firm, Blackhair, nothing will

harm you if you are not afraid. If you turn back you will lose your way."

"Sh," said his heart suddenly. "Keep still, Blackhair." He stood still and a stone's throw in front of him he saw a giant serpent.

"Run," cried his head. "Take cover, run as fast as you can."

"Keep still," warned his heart. "She will not harm you. If you run away she will see you." The serpent slid past without noticing him.

It must have been many hours later when he came to a rock, then another, then a third, and then so many that he could no longer count them.

The forest became lighter and in front of him stood a mighty stone statue. "There must have been a temple here once," thought Blackhair. "Yes," said his head, very quietly as if people were listening and it did not want them to hear. "Don't you remember your mother telling you about it? Many have come here and not returned. When evening comes the stones will come alive and your brave heart will stop beating. I tell you Blackhair, go back, go back, before it is too late." "Blackhair," said his heart comfortingly, "why are you afraid? This is the place." Then he lay down on the flat stones, stretched himself out and fell asleep. But his heart was awake and soon it began to beat so hard that it woke Blackhair up. "What is the matter, heart?" he asked.

"Take the gourd. The time has come," said his heart. Blackhair put it to his lips and drank the bitter water to the last drop. "Now you will die," shrieked his disappointed head. "You are brave," said his heart joyfully.

The night grew darker and darker. A jaguar howled in the distance and the great apes shrieked as they sprang from branch to branch. It was horrible.

Then something happened which made him forget his fear. The stones, the trees and the bushes began to dance and there was a humming and booming sound in the blue night sky which shimmered down on him through the giant branches. The stars came nearer and when he looked at the giant stones he felt he was nodding to them.

Then his feet began to get bigger. Longer and longer. For a moment his hand shone in the blue-green light and then his feet became gold as the sun and began to hurry through the forest. His stomach turned over.

He stumbled and fell lower and lower. He grabbed a branch with his hand. He heard a thunderous splintering sound as if a thousand trees were crashing down together.

He tried to cry out but his lips would not utter a sound.

He looked up. Wasn't that a ball of feathers coming out of his mouth? Then he was raised from the ground and flew through a golden gate. He was struck to the ground.

His head shrieked, with a thousand voices: "Shut your mouth or the feathered serpent will get out." Too late. Between his teeth a fiery red head appeared, slid out as he choked and vomited, and crept along the ground and up the stone wall. There she rested among her ruffled plumage and looked up at the sky.

"I am no longer afraid," thought Blackhair. He stood up and went up to the feathered serpent. "Who are you?" he asked. "I am Time," she said. "And where am I?" he asked again. "In the world of thoughts." "So there will be no more tomorrow for me?" "No." "And no yesterday?"

The serpent said no more. She opened her fangs and inside he saw the old medecine man. He was the colour of a glittering iguana, sea-green, and his eyes were blacker than the night. "Blackhair," he said, "I told you that you would find the right answer at the right time. Let your questions be like the wind. Everything flies before you. Let it come to you." The head disappeared and the feathered serpent closed its fangs. "Tell me, feathered serpent," called Blackhair, "how do I get to the kingdom of thoughts, where there are no more questions?" "Wait till the first rain falls which rises from the sea of diamonds," she said. "Come rain," said Blackhair, "from the sea of diamonds." The blue sky clouded over with flocks of clouds in splendid colours. They shimmered pale green and then the edges turned pink, as if a painter had painted round them with a fine brush. "Splish"–a drop fell on his back. Then "Splash," and this time one fell on his hand. "Where are you?" said Blackhair and felt about with his hand for the last drop that had fallen. "Here," said a small voice. Blackhair knelt down and looked for the raindrop from the sea of diamonds. But instead of the raindrop he found strewn carelessly on the ground the most beautiful garment made of gold and precious stones. He quickly forgot the poor raindrop. "I want this beautiful thing," he said, and took hold of it. It seemed that his wishes were faster than his thoughts, for while he was considering how he could best put it on, it was already on his body. They were no ordinary stones. They glittered with strange colours, shone like a thousand suns, went dim and grew bright again with a fresh brilliance. "If only my father or mother could see me, or even the old medecine man. They would be amazed."

"Blackhair," cried a voice from the fangs of the feathered serpent. "Have you come here

to dress up in finery? Haven't you something more important to do than look for treasure?" "What must I do, great serpent?" asked Blackhair. "Do not forget the raindrops," said the voice. He looked sadly down. But what was this? Was this the raindrop? How could he have forgotten it? It glistened and shone mysteriously like something magic.

Then it became bigger and bigger, until it was twice the size of Blackhair. "Here I am." it said, and it flew up like a humming-bird feather, and fell right on Blackhair. Suddenly he found himself sitting inside the raindrop, which was slowly going upwards. Beneath him the world became smaller and smaller. The forests looked like little tufts of colour on a carpet and the river like a pretty silver chain. He was not alone on the flight. From all directions came more little raindrops. The whole sky was full and there was a strange music everywhere, which grew very loud and died away mysteriously. Far below him shone the sea, a sea of diamonds. The drops glittered and each one reflected the whole world. Once he saw the moon, then a far-off star and then the sun dipped into the sea with a thousand golden hands and scattered the drops like bubbles. "Go on your journey," it said. "We will come back," the drops cried and flew high up into the sky. They kept bumping into each other and made a stranger and more beautiful sound than Blackhair had ever heard before. Forming a cloud, they flew over the earth and came to a high mountain. As if by a secret command, thousands of drops began to fall. Blackhair turned head over heels and fell swiftly down. He fell with such a bump that he bounded up again and crashed into some water. The water shook. The terrified raindrops sprang up into the air. Blackhair tried to get away–but it was too late.

Something seized him and pulled him to land.

"How did you slip in here?" thundered a voice. A giant finger as thick as the path through the fields in his village pointed towards him. Blackhair dared not move. He sat a prisoner in his drop of water. A guard decked in feathers held him in his hands like a glass ball. "I asked you," thundered the voice again, "how you got here." Blackhair leapt out of the drop of water wishing he could disappear into a cleft in the earth. Quick as lightning the giant hand caught him. "Did you try to vanish?" boomed the voice. The giant closed his fist on him and lifted him terrifyingly towards his mouth, which was full of sharp teeth. "So," said the giant, "and now will you tell me how you got here?"

14

Blackhair could hardly speak for terror. "I want to go to the kingdom of Mescal," he said bravely. "So you want to go to the kingdom of Mescal?" laughed the giant, becoming more friendly, "but do you know that that is dangerous? I am one of the many guards set to keep you out. The way leads through the kingdom of thoughts. You will find there everything that human beings have ever thought. Do you remember me sending you the golden robe? My servants will also try to tempt you and lead you astray. But if you escape them, the door to the kingdom of Mescal will stand open before you."

When he had finished speaking Blackhair was alone again. He saw four roads leading to the four corners of the sky, and a voice came from each direction. "This way, Blackhair. This is your way." "No, Blackhair, this way." It made him quite confused. At last he heard someone coming and he saw a man. "Come," the man said, "I will take you with me. I can run three thousand miles in one breath. No one will see you if I hurry away with you and here," he opened a bag, "here you can rest." "Thank you," said Blackhair, "but I want to go on alone." The man laughed. "You want to go on alone? Tell me, little man, when do you want to reach your goal? In three thousands years? Or do you want to wander forever, on your tiny ant-like legs?" He laughed and slapped his belly, because he found Blackhair so funny. After a while Blackhair came to a river. An old fisherman looked as if he was waiting for him. "Do you want to get over the water?" he asked cunningly. "Get in, I will bring you to the other bank." "Do not answer him," warned his heart and Blackhair went past. "I will swim over," he thought. But hardly had he set foot in the water when it began to bubble and boil. Horrible reptiles raised their heads and huge water serpents hissed threateningly. He ran away in terror and sank down tired and hopeless upon a stone.

"Blackhair," whispered a friendly voice. He listened but saw no one. "Blackhair," it whispered again. "Where are you?" he asked. "Here under your foot." He carefully lifted his foot and a tiny ant crept out. "Oh, it's you," said Blackhair disappointed. "Yes," said the ant. "Do you think that because I am so small I cannot help you?" "You should trust him," said his heart. "Take cover quickly," advised the ant, "for soon the reptiles and the giant serpents will come and sun themselves on the bank. When it grows dark wait for me at the top of the palm tree."

Then he heard the giant animals snorting and groaning. He ran as fast as he could to the palm tree and climbed up it. One reptile after another crept out of the water and lay

down under the tree. "Aaargh," snarled the giant jaws. The water serpents hissed and a thousand angry eyes looked up at the anxious Blackhair. He dared not move and the time went so slowly that he was in despair.

When the sun went down he heard the rushing of wings. "It is I," said a bird with the voice of the ant. Blackhair climbed fearlessly on to his back and hung on to his feathers. The bird flew higher and higher. He flew over the wide river, over mountains and valleys until the wind stopped singing. "Now we are there," said the bird joyfully. Blackhair slid off his back and the bird said: "Carry on this way. It is a difficult journey but it leads to your goal."

"Thank you, brother." Blackhair wanted to say, but the great bird had already gone. The way led through a land which looked like a sea of clouds full of strange lights. In the middle stood a fountain which shimmered with all the colours of the rainbow. It began to sparkle, and what looked like thin clouds of mist rose from it. A pale face looked out and then a hand rose up as if it were dancing. Then there were more faces and more hands. They came towards Blackhair swaying noiselessly out of the water. "What do you want?" he asked. But the silence continued.

Golden horns came out of the mist and Blackhair saw a cow looking at him with mournful eyes. A figure wearing a golden cap and the finest garments approached from the hills. He got on the cow's back and blew a flute. "Everything comes, everything passes. Forever coming and going, everything scatters . . ." sang the flute.

Soon Blackhair saw other animals, little tapirs and strange birds he had never seen before. And there was a horse resting on the clouds that let Blackhair stroke its neck.

"Clink, clank." He heard a noise below him. It was a man playing with golden coins. They flew up as if they were feathers, floated round him, fell again, changed colour and shone a pale silver when they hit each other. "What are you doing with the gold?" asked Blackhair in amazement. "Alas," said the man, "I am afraid of losing it and so my whole life has become a burden to me." "I know a way out," said Blackhair encouragingly, "beyond those hills everything can be forgotten." "What!" shrieked the man in a fury, "What shall I do there and what will happen to my gold? No, no, robbers will get it, the wind will carry it away."

"Then I cannot help you," said Blackhair sadly and went away. He continued along the path that led to the hills. Now and then he met other creatures going the same way in

silence. A little man sat on a donkey with a hundred legs. He had an enormous head, on which he wore a crown, but his hands and feet were small and delicate. His whole body seemed to have grown out of the giant head. "Think of your gold," shrieked the little man and swung his long whip. "Think of the thieves and the robbers who are waiting for you to fall sound asleep. Think of tomorrow. Are you prepared for it? What could happen tomorrow? Tomorrow the world may end and you may die. You may fall ill tomorrow, pine away or become poor . . ." Many of his companions turned back. "Who are you?" asked Blackhair in amazement. "I?" said the little man laughing. "I am the Emperor of Worries." "And what do you do?" "The questions you ask." He laughed again and cracked his whip. "I want to send everyone back who does not belong here."

At that moment the earth shuddered beneath them. An enormous herd of cattle went past followed by men on swift horses with flying hair. "Look," laughed the Emperor of Worries, "how they chase their desires, yet they will not even catch a single bullock." Then followed a rider with his lance down. "Look at that fool," cried the Emperor of Worries and cracked his whip. "He chases after danger and does not find it. I have known him for three ages of the world. And now go," he told Blackhair, "I want to keep tomorrow back and also your questions. If you go your way without desires you will learn everything for yourself. But beware of desires." He gave a friendly nod with his huge head and started the donkey's many legs moving and rode away. Far away Blackhair heard him calling again, "Think of your gold . . . Think of tomorrow . . ." The road became wider. More and more people came, there were animals nodding their grey heads, and giant birds flying above. Now and then a huge elephant moved clumsily among the other pilgrims. Guards from the great mountain, dressed as merchants, stood at the corners offering people carpets, splendid garments, or cool drinks under scarlet sunshades. A red haired man was showing a group of pilgrims a raven. "He has the gift of prophecy," he cried in a loud voice and many people gathered round. One wanted to know whether he would become rich soon, another asked how long he would live, another for the blessing of children and many other things. The nearer they came to the hills, the thicker became the crowd. The merchants and jugglers increased in number until the road ended in a wide meadow where people were lined up in rows. Many pilgrims forgot their goal for there were so many strange things for them to feast their eyes on.

A man with a green velvet turban stood on a board and beat incessantly upon a drum. Then a monkey beat the drum, and a goat with red eyes blew coloured balls into the air. Many people gathered round the juggler's tent. He beat again so hard upon the drum skin that four birds fell dead from a tree on to the drum. "These birds were killed by the sound of my drum," said the man. He bent down and picked up one of the dead birds and lifted it up. "Look," he said, "now it is . . ." "A serpent," shrieked the people. "Now an ox's horn," said the juggler. And indeed a smooth ox's horn lay on the palm of his hand. Nothing more was seen of the bird. "Step inside now," he cried and pointed with his stick to a black hole in a striped curtain . . . "It costs nothing but the trouble of taking a look." The people crowded in. There was no other way out of the tent. Blackhair saw no-one leaving it. "Strange," he said to himself and drew the curtain aside.

A hand pushed him from behind. "What is this?" screamed Blackhair and tried to defend himself, but the hand gripped him like a crab's claw. "At last I have got you," said the man in the turban joyfully. "I must go on," cried Blackhair. But the man sat him on a silk embroidered cushion. "Now," he said, "answer my questions." He sat down opposite him and said: "As to the number of numbers, have you counted the number of numbers or not?" Blackhair did not understand what the man meant. The man in the turban asked the same question again. "I don't know what you mean," said Blackhair hopelessly. "So," said the man, "you don't know what it means; I will ask you again: as to the number of numbers, have you counted the number of numbers or not?" When Blackhair still did not know what to answer, the man's eyes glinted nastily. Then the light went out and he saw only those glinting horrible eyes. They became enormous and then grew small again, and every time they changed he heard the same question: "As to the number of numbers, have you counted the number of numbers or not?"

Then Blackhair heard a familiar voice behind him. "I have come to help you for the last time. You were nearly seduced by the splendid robe, they tried to stir your desires in the dream market and distract you from your way, and now you are being mystified by empty words. These are the three forms of enchantment. You have to escape."

Now Blackhair breathed freely and his heart leapt for joy and he began to laugh. The hideous eyes went dim, the light came back and there was nothing more to be seen of the juggler.

Now the trees ran in front of Blackhair as if they wanted to show him the way to the kingdom of Mescal. When they came to a mound they stopped and as Blackhair went past them, they bowed their leafy heads to the ground and whispered: "Welcome." The darkness lifted and a tender light covered the landscape. Blackhair gave a cry. He saw thousands of domes. Buildings rose in front of him which were so beautiful that he had to close his eyes.

The windows of the towers and palaces glittered as if heaven and hell had met. Scarcely had he set eyes on one wonderful palace when another arose. There was a sound of water, ebbing and flowing like waves breaking on the shore, an everlasting creation which made all earthly strivings seem like mere bubbles. Pilgrims from many strange lands had reached the gates of the city. Some were almost naked, dressed only in loin cloths with long hair down to the ground. They sat quietly and humbly, with their legs crossed, at the gates where the streets ended. Others were clothed in shining yellow robes, some had orange cloaks with shawls held under their arms. There were also men with many-coloured turbans like the ones Blackhair had seen in the dream market and cloaked figures under brown or black hoods. There was a peasant with a wide straw hat, his face covered with innumerable wrinkles. A donkey-man whispered to a man in a yellow robe.

The door was opened. A light brighter than lightning streamed out and killed all the colours in the waiting crowd. Nothing now distinguished them. It was impossible to tell the difference between men and women, between a man in a yellow robe or one in a brown cloak, between young men and men of a hundred. There was no pushing and shoving as there had been in the dream market. No-one spoke as one after another they went in through the gate. Many had their eyes closed, others stumbled because they had never seen such glory. Before them went a man who took no notice of the splendour and walked the streets as if he knew them well. Blackhair stared at him in wonder and he heard someone whisper: "He knows the way to the goal of all goals."

A gust of wind recalled Blackhair from his dream. He looked up and saw a many coloured cloud – the cloud of evil thoughts. Out of every colour peered a horrible ugly face.

As the great crowd of pilgrims reached one of the palaces, clenched fists were raised against them out of the clouds. Then the faces opened their mouths and spat down deadly arrows upon the pilgrims. As the arrows rained down a terrifying figure sprang out of the palace with hundreds of arms and legs. He stamped his foot and there was a noise

like all the drums in the world beating together. And then he sang: "Hate falls upon hate, evil upon evil. I am the dancer of the law fulfilling the working of all things so that each man may meet with his own deeds."

And then he danced, throwing up his thousand hands, catching arrow after arrow. It was like a game, with the terrible dancer not letting one single arrow escape. The faces in the clouds gave a cry like thunder when they saw their deadly gifts disappearing into the dancer's quiver. He stopped dancing and reached out with his thousand arms and each one found an arrow. There was a horrible silence. The muscles stretched and then the arrows sped with a hissing sound after the escaping cloud faces. The arrows struck. A cry from a thousand mouths sounded horribly from the cloud. Not content with this, the merciless dancer attacked again until all the arrows in the quiver had been shot. Beyond the wall the faces fell out of the clouds. They fell with an angry roar and tried in vain to escape the destruction which surely awaited them. The fearsome dancer disappeared into the darkness of the temple.

In front of the temple Blackhair saw a man sitting under a blossoming tree. He wore a patchwork garment and was listening intently to the song of the crickets. A blossom fell on his lap. Carefully he lifted it up to the moonlight. He gazed out to sea and his thoughts wandered to the places where mankind lives. "If only I could tell you of my happiness," he said, "of a night when the crickets sang to me and the tree gave me its fairest blossoms. How rich I am and how seldom a beggar comes to me to whom I can give alms."

A path led through a temple where musicians were playing conch horns, and many hands beat diligently on big and little drums. A light just bright enough to throw a shadow flared up, and from a side door came a graceful dancer decked in coloured feathers. Her arms and legs were innumerable. Her hands traced a shape on the ground and then she laid upon it a horrible dragon's head. When she had done this she danced round the shape. Once she stroked the hideous head, then she nodded and sprang upon the slimy body. "Come, now come," she said, her hands beckoning. The monstrous shape arose. The drums beat loudly. A circle formed around the dancer but she did not lose her step. She spread her hands as if to defend herself from the monster. "Come, now come," she cried again. It hurried forward with its jaws open. It carefully followed every step and tried to find a weak point to dig in its claws. Then it showed its horrible teeth and growled.

Blackhair looked anxiously up to the shining dome of the temple. On a fragrant cherry blossom bough sat the Quetzal bird singing, singing so sweetly that Blackhair forgot everything else, the dancer, the monster and his gripping fear. And the bird sang, "He who loves selflessly is safe from envious claws." It became brighter and brighter and all of a sudden Blackhair found himself out in the street again as if nothing had happened. He saw few people about; he met only a splendid line of elephants. Before them rode riders on fiery horses and from the elephants' backs strangers nodded to him in a friendly way. The street led through gardens packed with flowers, in which the grass was like a carpet too precious to set foot upon. The blades did not grow straight up but were wavy and bent to form strange characters. There was a whispering sound in the shrubs and grasses and the branch of a tree called: "There he is. He is coming . . . Hush." And as he passed the secret whispering ceased. He saw water before him with silver birds swimming on it. Deep below there were fishes, motionless and colouring the water with the splendour of their scales. A swan glided across with open wings. It bent its neck and stared into the water. There was an island in the middle of the pond upon which many people were standing all looking at the bird. It turned its head to look at them and sang a melancholy song.

"That is the island of poets," said a pilgrim, "they honour the swan for it sings the most beautiful songs in the sea of sorrows."

Blackhair moved on, the swan's sad song following him until he came to a high wall. He looked in vain for a way through it, a door or a window.

"I will try and climb up it," he thought. But as if it had heard his thoughts, the wall grew as tall as the sky. He heard a sound and saw small stones rolling past his feet. They came quickly from all sides and began to form a ring. Two stones sprang into the circle, others gathered on the left, and the same number on the right, building themselves into a human form. It grew bigger and bigger. "Do you want to go to the palace with the thousand doors?" it asked. "Yes," said Blackhair. "Your desires bar your way," said the apparition. It shrank again and the stones hopped away. So Blackhair took no more notice of the wall and, free of desires, walked on happily until he came to a rainbow-coloured gate, which he went through.

There was the palace of Mescal, the palace of the thousand doors. One passage led to a door and on the other side a golden staircase led somewhere else. There was not just one

palace but a thousand or more, and arched gateways led from one splendid building to another. "Come my way," whispered the golden path. "You must climb the staircase," cried a voice from another direction. "Open this door here," said another. There were many voices, one from each of the many mysterious passages, staircases and archways. They became a choir and then a threatening stormy wind. He became confused and doubtful.

"Oh if only I could go back," he thought. Wherever he looked he saw innumerable domes, palaces and doors.

His head was drawing him in one direction and his heart in another. Then a voice said: "Open this door, for this is the right one." His head no longer protested and his heart beat so quickly that he could give it no answer.

"Blackhair," whispered a greyish figure, "where have you been all this time?" He stood still and the creature suddenly shrank. Its eyes became two slugs, its nose a bird, its mouth a red fish, its chin a snake and its hands swimming starfish. On its head sat a tortoise.

"This is the right door," his head and his heart cried together. The door flew open and the light was so bright that Blackhair had to shut his eyes. Before him stood a brilliantly coloured figure. Blackhair prostrated himself and did not dare to raise his face from the ground.

"Blackhair," it growled from its terrifying mouth, "what do you want?" But Blackhair could not speak. Again it said, "Blackhair, what do you want? Why have you come to me, the Lord of Mescal and ruler of the thousand gates and doors?"

"Answer him," said his head.

"Pacify him," said his heart.

"You can ride on a sunbeam," said the Lord of Mescal, reading his thoughts, "for thirty thousand ages through the world of the gods, through the thirty thousand doors and gates, but you will not understand any more than I, for the brighter the light, the darker the shadows."

As he spoke he began to look less frightening.

"Shut your eyes," he said. They flew up into the air, so fast that Blackhair felt that his skin was burning. Then they stopped.

They stood on a mountain looking at a landscape in a bluish light. He saw no living

creature, plant or bird. "Where are we?" he asked. "On another star," said the Lord of
Mescal. Blackhair was still considering this when their journey began again. He was
curious and opened his eyes a crack. He felt giddy. Colours and bright patches were
rushing past. First everything looked violet and then crimson. Then it all stopped again.
They were in a strange world of pools and craters. Here and there he saw tender
green shoots. Clouds of steam rose towards the sky from gaping holes and it was raining,
like on earth. Then they went on.

"If you still had the serpent Time in you," said the Lord, as they stood on another
mountain top, "you would have to die and be born again as many times as there are drops
of water in all the seas in the world. It would take that long before you could stand
on this star with me."

Now they were going through burning gases. "I am afraid," cried Blackhair. The Lord of
Mescal took him in his arms and covered him with his hands. There was a hissing
sound and then the air was filled with noises high and low which harmonised into a single
melody. He saw a light through his slitted eyelids, although the Lord of Mescal was
protecting his face with his hands; and the light shone so bright that the whole of the sky
looked as if it was on fire. All the colours in the sky had merged together and the
nearer they came to the light the more Blackhair shuddered with fear. The music went
higher and came to an end with a peal of bells, and the figure of the dancer appeared
in the sky like a thin veil. "The Mother of Life is above everything," said the lord. As she
had in the temple, she caressed the void tenderly with her hands and there was a
growling reply from the darkness like all the thunder in the world. "That is the stars
speaking," whispered Mescal. "No," cried Blackhair, "my head is bursting, let us reach
our destination before my fears overcome me." "Destination?" said the lord,
laughing. "We have no destination. Here there is no beginning and no end. But in your
mouth you still have a bit of the feathered serpent's tail, the Serpent of Time."

"What shall I do with it?" asked Blackhair. "Spit it out." "But that is my tongue," said
Blackhair cautiously. "Quite right," said the lord. "It says words which here are
meaningless and make you afraid."

He carefully opened his hand and Blackhair felt as though he was sitting on a small island
in the middle of a rough sea.

"Come," called the dancing Mother of Life. Blackhair opened his mouth and his tongue

broke off and flew away like an arrow. The Mother of Life came towards him and in her eyes he read the challenge: "Do you dare go on?"

"Yes," he said, stepping towards her, and at the same moment he and she were merged into one. The cold stars shone bright again. A burst of music surged through the universe, filling it with a single force – the force which said "Yes" to the endlessly returning dance of life.

And suddenly Blackhair could understand what the stars were saying. He was not afraid of the noise any more. Bright dust fell past him, gathered into balls and became thicker and thicker. Suns appeared but the voice of the Mother of Life kept him from scorching death. Things came and went. There were no more questions, for he had no tongue to frame the words. That which was high went still higher and that which was low climbed up step by step. Blackhair heard a thousand songs. The specks of dust of eternal ages, coming to be and passing away, of worlds which had existed and long since vanished. He sank lower and lower until his foot felt something soft. Then he heard a voice above him: "Blackhair, ask your heart what it has to tell you." And his heart answered: "I would like always to agree with your head." And his head answered: "I would like always to agree with your heart." When his head had said this, Blackhair felt a hand leading him across a meadow. "Is it you, Lord Mescal?" he asked. "Yes," answered the lord, "and now listen. Whatever knowledge you have is barren and worthless unless you also have sympathy and loving kindness."

Blackhair was alone. He saw the wall in front of the palace and went through it. He hurried through the tree-lined streets and suddenly found himself amidst the noise and bustle of the dream market. But his heart was not afraid. All the splendour passed him by. At a place where the sea was raging and roaring he went down, deeper and deeper, until a wave caught him and carried him far out. Then he floated on a sunbeam over desert lands. He no longer listened, as he had once, to the whisperings around him, and was not afraid to jump down when the mountainous clouds beneath him opened. "Plop," he landed on a leaf and fell smack on the head of the feathered serpent on the wall of the temple. He found himself growing larger and larger and when he tried to speak the feathered serpent jumped into his open mouth and would not keep still until the end of her tail had again become his tongue. Blackhair began to cry for he knew he could not tell anything about his journey into timelessness. It was horribly dark in the wood and

for the first time he heard the jaguar howling again. A snake slid through the bushes and in the water the tapirs grunted. Then he heard his head and his heart cry together: "He who loves selflessly is safe from envious claws." A tiny star shone through the thick roof of leaves. Blackhair got up and began to dance, like the Mother of Life, and he was no longer afraid. Then he sat down in the dark of the night, crossed his legs and lifted his eyes up to the burning light in the sky. He stood up and set out for home. He wandered the whole night, and in the morning when the sun shone here and there through the trees, he heard the Quetzal bird cry: "He is coming home, loaded with rich gifts." The tapirs led him to the edge of the fields, pushing the undergrowth aside to smooth his path. In the maize fields the peasants stood watching. "He is coming," they cried and ran before him. His father was making nets in front of the house, his mother was weaving and singing at her work. "I am back," said Blackhair. Their joy knew no bounds and all the people in the village gathered in front of his father's house. "What was it like?" asked one. "What happened to you?" asked another. "Were there spirits?" asked a third. And there were so many voices that none could be distinguished from the others. "I cannot speak yet," said Blackhair, "first I must have time to think it over."

Then Blackhair saw the Mother of Life, dancing in the sky, and heard the music of the heavens. He remembered the many doors of the palace of Mescal and saw its splendour reflected in the morning dew in the fields. He learned to understand the man full of hatred and to calm his anger. He could look deep into the heart of the envious man and make him ashamed And when people were sad and sunk in darkness he showed them the tiny light high up in the sky and taught them the dance of the Mother of Life. His fame spread abroad and pilgrims came to see him in his cabin which was open to all men and beasts. To all those who had ears to hear and eyes to see he showed the way to the palace of the thousand doors belonging to the Lord of Mescal. He gave them the key to men's hearts which is loving kindness and that clarity of mind which would help them to find the right way. He possessed nothing, but people called him the richest of men.

The Kingdom of Mescal, a legend from the Indians of Central America, appeals to people of very different temperaments, culture and belief. In this fairy tale for adults, told by Georg Schäfer and illustrated by Nan Cuz, herself an Indian, the pictures with their brilliant colours and simple lines and the patterns of speech with their engaging spontaneity combine to make a remarkable document of human belief, a book which is also a work of art.

The text is based on ancient Indian symbolic forms and tells the story of a boy who longs to get behind the appearance of things. A magic drink given to him by a medecine man sends him on a wonderful journey to a place where "the tongue forms no more words," into the depths of himself and to the heights of sheer wonder at the brilliance of the absolute. But such phrases as "magic drink," "journey" or "trip", "the depths of himself," have a far wider currency than that of the Indian world alone. The book is the story of the kind of journey described by Aldous Huxley in *The Doors of Perception;* and the man who goes through the door in the wall never comes back the same.

The rediscovery of drugs used in the religious cults of the past such as mescalin and nanacatl–a toadstool which causes brilliantly coloured dreams–and the synthetic substance commonly known as LSD, has aroused great public interest. Some approve of them, others stress their dangers. And the danger does exist of letting these drugs, whose secrets were so closely guarded in the past by a priesthood, become in our completely different society a form of consumer goods. Uncontrolled "trips" may be physically or psychologically harmful. Men of all times and places have wanted to escape the stresses of everyday life. The most widely used oriental drugs, opium and hashish, have much the same function in the East as alcohol does for the Westerner. But the Indian soma and the various American Indian drugs have another purpose. They are part of a highly developed cult which has nothing to do with mere intoxication. Magic drinks, particularly mescalin, are used in American Indian society as a means of spiritual transformation. They are thought to extend the consciousness, open the closed doors of the self and increase the richness of the soul.

Georg Schäfer and Nan Cuz experimented with synthetic mescalin shortly after the war. They discussed their findings in a scientific paper entitled "Experimental research on the time-space problem," which led to a correspondence with Albert Einstein. In *The Kingdom of Mescal* their researches have born a different kind of fruit, and art and literature are the richer for it.